A SHOT IN THE DARK

by Anne Schraff

Perfection Learning® Corporation
Logan, Iowa 51546

Cover Design: Mark Hagenberg

Cover Image Credit: Photodisc (Royalty-free)

For information, contact:
Perfection Learning® Corporation
1000 North Second Avenue, P.O. Box 500,
Logan, Iowa 51546-0500.
Phone: 1-800-831-4190 • Fax: 1-800-543-2745
perfectionlearning.com

Paperback ISBN 0-7891-6671-2
Reinforced Library Binding ISBN 0-7569-4767-7

1 2 3 4 5 6 PP 10 09 08 07 06 05

1 "HE HAD TO BE in the wrong place at the wrong time," Carla Rodriguez said to her boyfriend, Don Saenz, between classes.

They were remembering a month back to that warm night in September when Don's older brother, Julio, had been struck by a bullet and killed outside the Colorado Taco Shop on Madison Avenue. The police investigation was still under way, but everybody knew that solving the murder was getting more and more difficult as time went by. Trails were turning cold, and clues were becoming stale. At first everyone who didn't know Julio Saenz had said it was a gang shooting. Nothing unusual about that. There had been five so far this year. The neighborhood had many nice families and good people, but it also had its share of graffiti-scarred fences and buildings, of gangs fighting their wars in the night.

But Julio had just started attending State University, with dreams of going on to medical school. He had been valedictorian at Arturo Moreno High School, where he had graduated just four months earlier. Julio was not involved with gangs.

"Some gang members were shooting at each other, and he got mistaken for somebody else," Carla said.

"I can't believe that," Don insisted. "It was such a clean shot. They got him with one bullet, like a hit." Even now, weeks after it had happened, Don's voice broke as he talked about it.

Julio had been not only Don's big brother; he had been Don's hero. Don was now a junior at Moreno High, and after he graduated he planned to follow Julio to State. All through his life, even way back when he was struggling to get the training wheels off his bike and ride like the big guys did, Julio was showing him how, encouraging him. Don had often felt as if he were walking through a deep snowfield. But it hadn't been hard because his brother's big footsteps were up ahead to step into, tracks Julio left for him to make it easier.

"But nobody could have killed Julio on purpose," Carla said. "Everybody loved

Julio. He didn't have an enemy in the world. It had to be some kind of a mistake."

Right after Julio's death, after the big funeral at Our Lady of Guadalupe Church, where they couldn't fit in all the people who had attended, Don thought about his brother constantly. He couldn't concentrate on anything else. Even at his job at Harvey's Furniture Store, which he'd taken after Julio died, he thought of nothing but Julio.

Why? he kept asking himself. Why Julio? It seemed so wrong, so unjust. Julio was one of the good guys. Why him? Don tortured himself with the questions he could not answer. Sometimes he got so angry he could barely even function.

Now Don sat in history class and listened to Mr. Foxworth talk about World War II. The events seemed ancient to Don, but he tried his best to concentrate because Julio would want him to do his best even now.

Don't make me look bad, hermano mejor, Julio would always say with his famous grin that went from ear to ear. Julio was not only proud of his own efforts and determined to do his best, but he wanted his family to excel too. *Hey, Padre,* he would say to their dad, *no brown socks with black slacks. You want people to say the Saenz clan has no style?* Then he would roar with laughter and make everybody else laugh too.

"Pretty soon the whole world was engulfed in the war," Mr. Foxworth was saying, "the little war that everybody thought would stay in Czechoslovakia. Just toss a few Czechs to Hitler and he'd be satisfied. Yeah, right! So we all stuck our heads in the sand, and pretty soon we found out you can't stop a fire by pretending it's not burning."

Don thought about that for a few minutes. Whoever killed Julio was like a monster in the *barrio.* He had to be stopped, not only because the death of Julio had to be avenged, but also because the monster would kill again. The police had a lot of other crimes to investigate, though, including some other unsolved murders. They couldn't spend all their time and resources on finding Julio's killer.

But Don could help. He knew the *barrio.* He had lived there all his life. Someone must have information that could help the police.

Don thought of the apartment house for senior citizens across the street from the Colorado Taco Shop. Maybe some elderly person had been looking out the window at just the right time and had seen something. The police had already talked to the occupants, but sometimes people didn't talk to the police as honestly as they might talk to a kid looking for his brother's killer. Or maybe the very person the police missed was the one who saw something important.

Maybe Don would find some middle school kids who had seen the car speeding away from the taco shop and perhaps recognized the driver. Anything was possible.

Maybe a witness was keeping quiet out of fear. Maybe the person didn't want to rat out a cousin or a friend. But perhaps Don could get through to that witness, make him or her see what a wonderful life had been cut short that night in September, how many beautiful dreams died with Julio Saenz.

Or maybe, Don thought, it was all stupid.
Maybe he was an idiot to think he could do
the police's work.

....

After school, Don walked home to the
old stucco house where his family lived,
his mind churning in the usual paths. It was
now just him, his 10-year-old sister, and
their parents. Julio was just one person,
and yet his loss had torn a huge gaping
hole in the family. Now a cruel, raw wind
was howling through their souls. When
Julio was alive, he and Don had shared a
good-sized bedroom. Their mom and dad
had the largest bedroom, and 10-year-old
Josefina had the little bedroom to herself.
Now Don had a bedroom to himself too.
But his mom kept Julio's desk in there,
bearing a photograph of him with a vigil
candle burning day and night.

Each family member was handling their
sorrow in different ways. Don's dad, who
was a mechanic at the local Chevrolet
dealership, was putting in all the overtime
he could. He was determined to be so busy
during all his waking hours that he would

not have even a second to cry for his lost son. When he finally got home from work, he wolfed down his supper and then fell into bed in a stupor-like sleep. Julio was his dad's firstborn. Even though his dad loved all his children, there was always a special bond between him and Julio.

Don's mom now went to Mass every morning at Our Lady of Guadalupe Church. Before, she had attended faithfully on Sundays, but now it was every morning. She said that now that her baby had crossed over to the other side, she felt closer to him at church than anywhere else. She had last seen Julio in church, so handsome with white satin around him, his hands closed around a rosary. His mom put red roses before the picture of Our Lady of Guadalupe every day—red roses for Julio.

Josefina, always a chatterbox, had grown strangely quiet. She continued to be a good student as she always was, but she didn't seem interested anymore in clothes, her cheap little trinket jewelry, or music. Don worried about Josefina. She used to laugh and make stupid jokes all the time, and now she scarcely smiled.

Whoever had killed Julio had not only taken his life but had dramatically changed the Saenz family too.

"Hey, Don!" A familiar voice made Don slow down. It belonged to Matt Garcia, his best friend at Moreno High. They both played football, but Matt was the better athlete.

"Hey, Matt," Don said.

"You're walking awful fast, man," Matt said. "You in a hurry to get home?"

"No. Nobody there anyway. My mom's probably in church, and my dad will be working until it's dark. Josefina's with a friend this afternoon," Don said.

"I was talking to some guys," Matt said, "and they said they saw Rattler hanging around the Colorado Taco Shop the afternoon of the day Julio was shot."

Don stiffened. Rattler's real name was Ric, but he was such a snake that everybody called him Rattler, even his friends. He liked it too. He thought it gave him more power to intimidate, which was his main game.

"Who says?" Don asked.

"Neal Harvey," Matt said. Neal was

the son of the man who owned Harvey's Furniture Store, where Julio had worked for almost a year and where Don now worked, doing his brother's old job. "Couple other guys with Neal saw Rattler too."

Don had never heard Julio talk about having any trouble with Rattler. Julio was such a good-natured guy, he could kid the worst enemy out of his hostility. Not that he ever tried with Rattler. He just avoided the guy. "So, they say Rattler was just hanging around there?" Don asked.

"Yeah, looking things over," Matt said.

Don recalled the day his brother was shot in excruciating detail. It was an ordinary Friday, a school day. Don remembered Julio talking about the Moreno Mastiffs football team and how he thought they had a good shot at making the playoffs this year. Even though Julio was in college, his class schedule allowed him to attend football practice at Moreno to give his moral support to his brother and his old buddies.

Was it possible that Julio had some sort of a problem with Rattler and he just kept it to himself? Julio was pretty cool.

He liked to handle his own problems and not worry other people with them. But Don remembered his brother avoiding gang members like Rattler all his life. Why would he have suddenly gotten mixed up with Rattler?

Still, now that Don thought about it, Julio *had* seemed quieter and more preoccupied that Friday morning than he usually was. Maybe something was on his mind.

Neal Harvey was captain of the football team, a big, friendly kid who was pretty popular. Moreno High School was about one-third Hispanic, one-third black, and one-third Asian and white. The kids got along real well, but the economic status of the various groups was very different. The students from the *barrio* and surrounding neighborhoods were lower- and middle-class, but a new development that stretched into the woods had recently popped up, and the houses there were very pricey. That's where the Harvey family lived. Even though his father had a lot of money, Neal was pretty down-to-earth. He worked at his father's furniture store, mostly in the office. The other kids who worked there, like Julio and Don, hauled heavy furniture around and loaded the trucks that took appliances and living room sets out to the customers. Some of those kids abhorred a kid like Neal who got such a cushy job, but Don didn't hate him for it. He was the boss's son. What did anybody expect?

"I think I'll go talk to Neal. Maybe I'll see Rattler too," Don said. "I really want to help the police find out who killed Julio. I think about it all the time. It's making me crazy to know that his killer is out there walking the streets, enjoying burgers and fries, watching baseball, and going to the movies. Sometimes I think of it in the middle of the night, and I want to get up and run down the street like a madman. I feel like knocking on doors and dragging people out of their beds, asking them if they're sure they never saw anybody kill my brother that night. It just keeps playing over in my mind like a terrible movie—getting the news that he was hit, going down to the hospital, and seeing the doctors shake my dad's hand and say they were sorry but they did all they could. It's like Julio was killed yesterday. The wound is still that raw, man."

"Yeah," Matt said. "It has to be rough. But be careful when you talk to Rattler. I think he's the most evil dude I ever saw."

That night, as Don ate dinner with his family, conversation was sparse. His dad said something about fixing a Corvette at the garage. His mom asked everybody if the cheese enchiladas were all right or if anybody wanted more salsa. Josefina said she got another A in math, but nobody seemed as excited as they used to be about such an announcement. Josefina went back to eating her dinner.

....

On Saturday, Don didn't start work at Harvey's Furniture Store until afternoon, so he had time to climb into his pickup and drive over to the part of town where Rattler lived. Don didn't tell his parents he was going to talk to Rattler. His mom and dad wouldn't want Don doing any investigating on his own. Don could just hear his mother's anguished voice if she knew about it. *Don! I have lost one son already! What are you thinking of? I cannot bear to lose another son. Don't go near that bad man!*

Don knew that Rattler lived with a couple of his cousins in a rundown apartment building at the end of a dirt street. The Dumpsters around there always overflowed with old mattresses and other debris, but Rattler always had a shiny new car. He had a lot of jewelry too, and he flashed wads of bills.

Don parked near the apartment building and walked up the dirt road as a pair of pit bulls yapped at him. As he was walking toward the door, he spotted Rattler standing by his new car with two friends. All three of them glared at Don as he approached.

"What's your problem, man?" Rattler called out. "Only my friends come down that road. You go back to that junk truck of yours and hit the road."

"Remember me, Rattler? I'm Don Saenz, Julio's brother," Don said.

"So what? So you're a dead guy's brother. What's that to me?" Rattler snapped. His friends laughed. "Say what you came to say and get lost, man."

"I heard that the afternoon of the night my brother was shot, you were seen looking around the Colorado Taco Shop on Madison," Don said. "Did you have something against my brother?"

Rattler's already hostile face turned angrier. "I go anywhere I want anytime I want, and I don't answer to anybody. I don't answer questions from little zit-faced punks either."

"I just want to know if there was bad blood between you and Julio," Don said.

"You know what?" Rattler asked in a mocking voice. "Guys like him never got my attention—stupid dudes who stuck in school and sat in classrooms listening to idiot teachers."

The other two men laughed again, almost on cue, as if Rattler expected an appreciative audience.

Don felt the anger creeping up his neck, turning it ruddy. He wanted to grab Rattler by the shoulders and shake him like a cat shakes a mouse. Don wanted to shake the truth out of him and wipe that evil smile off his nasty face.

But then Don might have to deal with the sharpened screwdrivers Rattler's two friends were twirling.

2 THEN DON SPOTTED the girl in the car. Elena Redondo was about a year older than Don. She had dropped out of Moreno High School when she was 16, the same time she started hanging around Rattler. Her life went downhill fast. The last time Don saw her, she had been beautiful. She had long, lustrous black hair, sparkling dark eyes, and a warm, happy smile. When Don was a freshman at Moreno, he thought she was just about the prettiest girl he'd ever seen. Now she looked weary and scared. When her gaze met Don's, a tiny, wan smile of recognition flickered there.

Don didn't say anything else to Rattler. He had not gone there expecting the truth. He just thought he might find a clue in Rattler's body language, but he didn't. The guy was ice cold. As Don walked away, he heard Rattler and his friends trailing his steps with their jibes and laughter.

Don drove over to Carla's house. Whenever he was feeling low, she could pick up his spirits. Now he was feeling so low he thought a dark cloud must be hovering over his head.

"Want to go for a burger?" Don asked Carla. He didn't like Mexican food as much as the rest of his family did. He needed a burger and fries now and then.

"Sure," Carla said. As they drove to the burger place, Don told her about seeing Rattler.

"Oh, Don, what a big *bobo* you are going over there! You go right into his nest and dis him when his friends are there? What's the matter with you?" Carla said.

"I didn't dis him. I just asked him if he had a problem with Julio. Matt told me some guys saw Rattler hanging around the Colorado Taco Shop the day Julio was shot. Guess who else I saw? Elena Redondo. She looked like something the cat dragged in," Don said.

"Yeah," Carla agreed. "Her sister goes to State, and she's doing good. Julio was trying to get Elena to get her GED so she'd have some kind of a life."

Don turned his head sharply and looked at Carla. "Julio was trying to help Elena?

He never told me that," he said.

"You know how Julio was. You show him a sick puppy and he's trying to make it better," Carla said. "He was mostly talking to Elena's sister at State and trying to get her to push Elena into doing the right thing. With a GED, she'd at least have a chance."

"Maybe that's what got Rattler mad at Julio," Don said. "Maybe he thought Julio was messing with his girlfriend."

"Yeah, he's really jealous," Carla said. "He hits Elena. If she even looks at another guy, he smashes her in the face. That girl is *estupido*! If a guy ever laid a rough hand on me, he'd be the sorriest *hombre* around."

Don recalled the sad little smile Elena cast him. Maybe she knew something about what happened to Julio. Don decided he would try to catch her alone. She still lived with her mother, sister, and brother in a little stucco house near Don's house. He planned to go over there and talk to her when Rattler wasn't around.

After lunch, Don said good-bye to Carla and headed to Harvey's Furniture Store. When he got there, Neal was in the office talking to his father. Neal was a little bit lazy and liked to fool around, and because he was the boss's son he got away with it.

Neal looked just like his father except for the wine-colored birthmark his father had on his left cheek. Neal had the same square shape, the same shape of head, small eyes, and a big forehead. Neal wasn't heavy yet like his dad.

When Don finished loading the truck with furniture, he came back inside to see Neal taking a coffee break.

"Hey, Neal. Matt told me you and some friends saw Rattler hanging around the Colorado Taco Shop the afternoon of the night Julio got shot. Is that right?" Don asked.

"Yeah," Neal said. "The guy gives me major creeps. He was just lurking around. I figured some gang stuff was coming down and that's why he was there."

"My brother Julio was never mixed up with gangs," Don said.

Neal had a funny look on his face, like it was hard for him to believe that any Hispanic boy was completely free of gang connections. But he shrugged and said, "Whatever. I don't know much about it. All

I know is Rattler was strutting around like he owned the street."

Mr. Harvey was very good about hiring Hispanic and black students, but still Don got the impression that he looked down on people with darker skin. It was as if he knew that moving heavy furniture out on the loading dock in the hot sun was no work for white kids, and he was glad there were dark-skinned students to do it for minimum wage. Not that Julio in his turn or now Don really held it against the guy. It was a job, and they needed the money.

"You didn't hear Rattler say anything that day, did you?" Don asked, fishing desperately for some scrap of information.

"No, we got out of there fast. None of us wanted to be anywhere near that guy and his kind," Neal said. He paused then and said, "You know, Don, I'm really sorry about what happened to your brother. I've wanted to tell you that."

"Thanks," Don said.

"I mean, he was a good guy. Everybody liked him," Neal said. "I know how hard it is to lose somebody like that."

Don thought, how do you know, man?

Have you ever lost a brother? Or anybody you cared about? But he just said, "Yeah."

"I, uh, understand how messed up your head gets when something bad like that happens," Neal continued. "I mean, it's like nothing is the same, like the whole world gets different and doesn't even look right anymore."

Don stared right at Neal, wanting to ask him how he knew, how he could even begin to know the terrible hurt inside Don's heart. Neal had a comfortable life, and everybody in his family was doing well. The biggest problem he had to worry about was whether to make the sirloin well done or rare tonight.

But then Neal answered the question in Don's mind without Don having to ask. "My parents split up, you know." He said it in a kind of offhanded way, like it didn't matter to him all that much. But as he spoke his lower lip trembled with emotion, and Don could see it was a pretty big deal after all. His voice broke too, betraying him. "My mom moved out a month ago. Just took off. Never even said good-bye to me. Not to anybody, I guess. I never saw it coming. I never even had a clue. It's so weird. One day she's kidding with me and making cookies, and the next day she's gone without a word."

Don was really surprised by the revelation. He didn't know that much about the Harvey family, but what he did know made him think they were an ordinary, uncomplicated family with more money than most people and a lot fewer problems.

"I didn't know your parents were having problems," Don said. "That's too bad."

"Yeah, well, I don't talk about it a lot. My dad doesn't talk about it either. He just works more, I guess. He's trying to lose himself in his work," Neal said.

Suddenly there was a bond between Neal and Don—a rich, white guy with a brand-new car given to him by his parents, and a Hispanic kid with an old truck limping along with 200,000 miles on the odometer and whose parents were struggling to make ends meet. Skin color and money suddenly meant nothing.

"You know," Don said, "my dad's the same way. Ever since Julio died, all he wants to do is work. He'd like to work all day and night, I think, just so there's no time to stop and remember that his boy is dead."

"Yeah," Neal said. "It's so weird around our house with my mom gone. Real weird, like there's some hole somewhere that you can't see; you can only feel it."

Don and Neal stood awkwardly for a silent moment. Then Neal returned to the office where his father was on the phone. Don moved some more furniture until it was quitting time. Then Don rushed out to his pickup and drove over to the green stucco house where Elena lived.

When Don knocked on the door, a boy that looked about 11 years old answered. Don asked, "Is your sister Elena home?"

"Uh-huh," the boy said.

"Tell her Don Saenz wants to see her. I'll wait out here," Don said.

The boy was gone for a few minutes, and then Elena appeared. She stepped outside, closing the door after her. Don figured she didn't want her mother to hear her talking about her boyfriend, Rattler.

"Hi, Don," Elena said. Don had not

talked to her since Julio's funeral. She and her family had gone to pay their respects.

"Elena, I'm not going to hassle you about hanging out with Rattler, even though I think it's really sad that a girl as fine as you is doing something so stupid. I just wanted to ask you if you knew of any bad blood between Rattler and my brother. Anything Rattler might have said?" Don asked.

"No," Elena said. "He never talked about Julio. I don't think he ever even thought about him. They had nothing in common. They moved in two different worlds. I never heard Ric even mention Julio's name."

"Julio wanted you to go back to school and get your GED, didn't he?" Don asked. "You think that might have made Rattler mad?"

"No, I never told him," Elena said. "He didn't know about it at all."

"Are you sure, Elena? He might've thought if you got your GED you'd be able to make something of yourself and then you'd leave him," Don said.

"Julio was mostly just talking to my sister about it," Elena said. "He hardly talked to me. My sister goes to State, and

Julio would run into her there and nag her to make me get my GED. Anyway, Ric is not as bad as some people say. He can be mean sometimes, but he's nice sometimes too."

"He hits you, doesn't he, Elena?" Don asked.

"Maybe once or twice, but I didn't have to go to the hospital or anything. Like he'll pull my hair or he'll slap my face, but he's never broken anything," Elena said.

"Elena, don't you realize how bad that is?" Don said. "No guy has the right to abuse a girl like that, not for any reason!"

"Don, I'm no angel either," Elena said. "Sometimes I do flirt with other guys, even though I know it makes Ric crazy. I think I love him, Don. Don't dis him like he's nothing. I really think I love him. He does bad things sometimes, but so do I. I'm not a very good girl, Don. I'm not sweet like Carla. But I'll tell you one thing, Ric didn't have anything to do with Julio getting shot that night. I swear he didn't. He would have told me something was going down, and he didn't. He didn't have anything against Julio. Nothing. When Ric has something against a guy, when he hates him really bad, everyone knows it," Elena said in a high emotional voice. "But he never dissed Julio. Not once. I swear that's true, Don."

Don heard a car's brakes then, squealing in the dark. He turned and looked. At the same moment Elena cried, "Oh no! It's Ric. He's seen us!"

Elena spun around and ran back inside the house, leaving Don standing in the glare of the porch light. Don wished he were one of those moths circling the light over his head.

Rattler's car slowed to a stop in front of the house.

3 DON DIDN'T EVEN TRY to sink into the shadows. Rattler had seen him, and there was no getting away from it. It would just make matters worse for Elena if he tried to sneak off.

"What are you doing here, Saenz?" Rattler yelled from the passenger side of the car. Don could see that another man was driving.

"I don't have to answer to you about where I go," Don shot back. He had to act as tough as he could. If Rattler sensed fear or weakness, he went in for the kill.

"I got an interest in the lady who lives here, man," Rattler snarled. "You messing with my lady?"

Don felt like telling Rattler where he could go with his questions, but he didn't want to make big problems for Elena. So he casually walked up to Rattler's car and said, "I wondered if Elena had heard anything that would help us find Julio's killer. She didn't end up knowing anything, but I had to check it out, you know?"

Rattler seemed satisfied with the explanation, but he couldn't resist a parting jibe. "Man, you're too curious. You know what happened to the cat who got too curious?"

Don went to his pickup and took off. His blood was boiling. Rattler was like a dreaded disease in the neighborhood with his bullying and his threats. It infuriated Don that a guy like Rattler could terrorize so many people and get away with it. Even Mr. Harvey paid off Rattler.

"It's less expensive than replacing windows and fixing vandalism," Mr. Harvey had once said.

Rattler had been arrested a few times for minor things, but he never got in trouble for beating guys so badly they ended up in the hospital with their jaws wired shut or for throwing Elena—and Anita before her— against walls and bruising their bodies. He never got busted for the drugs he dealt or for the extortion he was working against the whole *barrio*.

And maybe he had gotten away with killing Julio. Don had no hard evidence yet, but he had a gut feeling that it was Rattler who had taken Julio out. He had to nail him and make him pay.

When Don got home, he found his little sister sitting on the front lawn flipping through a magazine. He could tell she wasn't really reading it. She often sat on the porch at night when it was still warm in the house and much cooler outside.

"Hey, Josie, how's it going?" Don asked, snagging one of her braids and giving it a playful twirl. Usually when he did that Josefina laughed, but this time she just pulled her braid back.

Josefina would not even look up at her brother.

Don knelt on the grass beside her and said, "Hey, *hermana*, what's the matter? Why are you being so grumpy?"

When Josefina finally looked up, Don saw that tears had made tracks down her cheeks. Josefina was the darkest of the three children, much darker than Julio had been and even darker than Don. She was very pretty with large brown eyes and a dimple in her chin. She was always the happy one in the family, making jokes and singing silly songs, even getting into mischief. Maybe it was because her parents wanted a little girl so badly and had worried they would have only boys. Julio and Don wanted a little sister too, so now everybody doted on her and forgave her for all of her pranks.

But now, clearly, she had been crying.

Don gently lifted Josefina's chin and asked, "What's the matter?"

"Ellie won't play with me anymore," Josefina said.

"Ellie Chandler, your best friend?" Don asked in shock. Ellie and Josie had been buddies since first grade. They spent their entire lives in and out of each other's houses. "Why won't she play with you?"

"Because her mom says we're bad people, and she won't let Ellie hang around with bad people," Josefina said.

"Josie, that doesn't make sense," Don said.

"Well, it's true!" Josie said, jumping to her feet. "I don't care, either. I don't like Ellie anymore. She's mean and stuck up!"

Don caught sight of their mother standing in the doorway. "Come on in, Josie," she said. "It's pretty cool in the house now. There's a nice breeze coming in the windows. I made you some flan, Josie. Come and eat it."

"I'm not hungry," Josefina said, running past her mother to her room.

Don stood there, looking at his mother. "Is it true what she said about Ellie? Won't her mom let her play with Josie anymore?"

"It's true," his mom said sadly. "When I walked out of the church this morning, June Chandler was waiting for me. She looked very sad and embarrassed. We have always been good friends, you know. She said it would be best if the girls didn't play together, at least for a while. I said, 'June, I don't understand. My little girl has just lost her brother, and now must she lose her best friend too? It will be so hard for her.' June looked down at the sidewalk, not even into my eyes. She said she was sorry, but it's her husband's decision. Her husband said we must be a gang family to have lost our son to gang violence, and he doesn't want to risk his daughter's life by letting her hang around a gang family."

"Mom!" Don cried. "Julio wasn't in a gang! I've never had anything to do with gangs either!"

"*Hijo*, you know this, and I know it. But Julio was shot down in the street like so many boys. Everybody is saying 'gang-related.' We are Mexican, so everybody just thinks, 'Oh, sure, yeah, it's gang stuff.'"

Don went into the house, his hands clenched in anger. It was so unfair! But then he thought about how the papers had reported the shooting. They were hinting at a gang connection immediately. They just assumed that was what happened. The local TV news programs talked about the police looking into the possibility that it was gang-related. That stuck in everybody's mind.

Don went to Josefina's room and knocked on the closed door. "It's me, *cosa dulce*," he said.

"You can come in if you want," Josefina said. "I don't care."

When Don walked in, Josefina was sitting in her rocker with an oversized beanbag monkey on her lap.

"I'm sorry about Ellie," Don said. "Her family is being really stupid. They think Julio was shot because he was a gang member, but he wasn't. He was a good, smart guy who was going to college to be a doctor."

"I don't care," Josefina said, her lower lip trembling.

"But we know the truth about Julio," Don said.

Josefina looked up, defiance in her eyes. "Maybe Julio did stuff we didn't know about. That's what Tyrone told me at school today. He said Julio was a goody-goody guy to his family, but when he was out on the street, maybe he was somebody else. He said maybe Julio wore gang colors like the other guys," she said.

"Josie, you know that's not true," Don said.

"Maybe," Josefina said. "But everybody at school thinks he was a gang member and so it doesn't matter. I mean, if everybody thinks you're a thief, then who cares if you are or not because that's what everybody thinks anyway."

Don walked over to his sister and knelt before her, taking her hands in his. "Josie, you know Julio was good. Don't spit on his memory by talking like this. Do you hear me? It's like killing Julio all over again to attack him with lies. Josie, those stupid people at school don't know what they're talking about. Some of them do bad things, and they want to think everybody else is bad too," he said.

Josefina started to cry again. "Listen to me, Josie," Don said. "You hold your head up high at that school, and you tell everybody that Julio was the best there was and you're proud of him. If somebody wants to believe bad things about our family, then they're the losers," Don said.

Josefina nodded. Don gave her a big hug then and left the bedroom. He went back to his own room, the one he had shared with Julio.

The room still contained a lot of Julio's stuff. Don didn't want to move it out. If he did that, it would feel as if he was trying to forget his brother, and he didn't ever want to forget Julio. Don gently picked up Julio's favorite jacket. As he did, a note fell from the pocket and fluttered to the floor.

Don picked up the typewritten note.

Julio—I can explain everything. It's not what you think. Leave the police out of it for now, please. I'll explain everything.

The note was unsigned.

A chill traveled through Don's body. Julio was not wearing his jacket the night he was killed, but he wore it often when he worked late at the store.

Don knew the police hadn't seen the note. Maybe it meant something. To Don, it meant one thing at least. Julio had been involved in something his family knew nothing about. And that was unsettling.

Don racked his brain now to remember the details of Julio's last week. Maybe something he had ignored at the time was really important. Was Julio under obvious stress and was Don too busy with his own activities to notice?

Don sat in the bedroom, sorting through Julio's desk. He felt funny doing it, even now after Julio had died. It seemed as if he was eavesdropping in his brother's life, violating his privacy. But of course, it didn't matter anymore.

Don found notes from Julio's college friends, unfinished term papers. Julio's checkbook. He found the car payment book for the used Honda Civic he had just bought, the sharp little car his dad had quickly sold because just looking at it made his heart ache.

There were letters in beautiful handwriting from Tami Ferraro, the lovely, sweet girl Julio had met, the girl who despised e-mail and absolutely would have nothing to do with it. Tami went to State College too, and she and Julio had been dating for about four months. She had taken a trip back East to see her grandparents, and she had written many letters to Julio. Don noticed a special twinkle in Julio's eyes when he talked about Tami. Don remembered her coming to the funeral, sitting in the last pew of Our Lady of Guadalupe Church, her face swollen from crying. Don scanned her letters. Some were a little gushy, but most of them were just newsy, filled with anecdotes about New York.

Don continued sorting through the material until he found Julio's appointment calendar. Julio had written in the dates of upcoming tests, his work schedule at Harvey's Furniture Store, and birthdays.

Don checked the entries for the final week—
an exam in western civ. on Monday, biology
project due on Wednesday. He worked
Wednesday, Thursday, and Friday.

Then Don saw the terse note.

"Friday, Colorado Taco, 9 p.m."

He had an appointment to meet
somebody at 9 p.m. at the Colorado Taco
Shop. He was shot and killed at 9:03. He was
going there to meet someone, and whoever
it was did not plan to talk to him. The
person planned to kill him, and Julio didn't
know it. It wasn't a random shot after all.
He wasn't at the wrong place at the wrong
time. It was a hit—a premeditated murder.

Don turned numb. It was so terrible to
contemplate that somebody, anybody,
had actually wanted to kill Julio. It was so
unbelievable given the kind of guy he was.

Don continued looking through the stuff,
almost feverishly now. He scanned all the
messages, even the ones written on the
backs of sales slips. He needed to locate
anything that the police could use, every
scrap that could contain a clue.

On one of the sales slips, Don came
across a note Julio had written to himself.

"Tami—Fri. nite. Beach." Did he have a date with Tami that night? Surely he wasn't meeting her at the Colorado Taco Shop. It was tiny—no place for a date. But no, he had written "beach." They must have planned to drive down to the ocean. Don remembered that Julio loved to sit at the water at night and watch the moonlight glisten on the throbbing waves. So Julio was meeting Tami Friday night, and someone else too . . .

Julio found the letter then. It had been printed out from a computer.

I'm all mixed up. I care for you a lot, but you seem to think I'm somebody you can jerk around, and that's not me. Let's just clear the air, okay? I can live without you, although it's going to hurt, but I can't live with this stupid lying and pretending and stuff like that. If we can't get together for real, then let's just call the whole thing off, baby.

Space Girl

Don stared at the letter, wondering what it had to do with Julio. Was Julio dating

two girls? Both Tami and this girl? Or was
Tami "Space Girl"?

4 DON FELT WEIRD calling Tami Monday morning. His mom had gone to Mass, and his dad had gone to work, dropping Josefina off at school on his way. Don decided to make the call before he left for school.

Don had seen Tami a few times. She had attended a family barbecue about two months ago when Don and his whole family were celebrating their *abuela's* 75th birthday. She seemed like a nice, quiet girl. And she was beautiful. She and Julio made a terrific couple. The last time Don saw her was at Julio's funeral. She had sat sobbing throughout the ceremony. He hoped she hadn't left for class yet.

"Hello?" a girl's voice answered.

"Hi. Is this Tami Ferraro?" Don asked shakily.

"Yes. Who is this?" the girl sounded tense.

"I'm sorry to bother you, but this is Don Saenz, Julio's brother," Don said.

"Oh," she said.

"I was wondering if I could talk to you," Don said.

"Talk to me? About what? What is this all about?" She sounded suspicious.

"I, uh . . . am talking to people who knew Julio, you know, just trying to see if I can't find out something to help the police figure out who killed him," Don stammered. "The police haven't gotten very far in solving it, you know. I'm just seeing if they missed anything, some important little clue. I thought maybe you might be able to help. If you had time to talk to me."

"I talked to the police," Tami said. "I don't know anything more than what I told them, which is nothing."

"But maybe you could meet me somewhere, like at the college, and we could just talk for a few minutes," Don suggested.

"I don't want to talk about what happened to Julio," Tami said emphatically. "I really don't even want to think about it. It just tore me apart. It was so terrible for me. Even though we hadn't dated that long, we were really close. We were even talking about the future. It was such a horrible shock. I don't want to think about it anymore."

"Well, could you at least tell me this—you had a date with him the night he died, right?" Don pressed on desperately.

"Yes, we were meeting at the Sandpiper Shed at 9:30," Tami said. "It was our favorite place on the beach. It's just a funky little restaurant. I was sitting there waiting, and he didn't come and he didn't come, and so I called your house and everybody was . . . screaming and crying. Somebody told me he was dead. Please, I don't want to talk about it anymore. I quit college over it. I'm taking a semester off to get my head together. It's the most terrible thing that has ever happened to me. I've never been close with anyone before who was . . . murdered. I have to go now," Tami said.

"I'm sorry I bothered you," Don said. "I'm just determined to find out who killed my brother. It's like an open wound in my heart."

"I'm sorry too," she said before she hung up.

When Don got to school, he tried to concentrate on his classes, but he kept thinking about the documents he would take to the police after school. He had made copies of the unsigned note, the woman's letter, and the entries in Julio's appointment book. Maybe none of them meant anything, but perhaps they would provide the missing link in the case.

Don ate lunch with Matt and Carla that day.

"You know, I thought I really knew my brother," he said, "I thought he was such an open guy and there were no secrets in his life. But I found some notes and letters, and I know that something was bothering him—something big."

"Yeah," Carla said. "Everybody is secretive about some things. There's stuff my mom and dad don't know about me, and if I can help it, they never will. I read somewhere that we spend our lives trying to find out who we are and we never find out who anybody else really is."

Neal walked up then carrying his tray. "You guys mind if I join you?" he asked.

"No," Don said. Neal was always a fairly nice guy, but usually he didn't hang with Don and his friends. He mostly sat with kids from his own neighborhood. Don was surprised that he wanted to sit there with three Mexican students. But immediately, Neal looked at Carla and said, "I heard what you were saying about not knowing people, even people real close to us. Man, is that ever true." Neal looked more vulnerable and shaky than Don had ever seen him.

"What's happening, Neal?" Carla asked.

"My mom left about a month ago," he said. "I knew she and my dad were fighting more than usual, but I thought maybe that happens to people. I didn't think she'd do what she did though. Just cleared out while I was at school. I mean, packed her stuff and just went. Never even said good-bye."

"Wow, that is awful," Carla said. "Was she mad at you or something? Like did you side with your dad when they were fighting? I always stay neutral when my mom and dad are at war."

"My mom and I were really close," Neal said. "I guess I always took her side. I mean, I thought she loved me a lot. I can't believe she won't even call me and tell me she's okay." Neal stared into his spaghetti, tears threatening to spill from his troubled eyes.

"What does your dad say about it?" Don asked.

"He's as confused as I am," Neal said. "He says my mom is at a time in life when women sometimes act weird. He thinks she just wants to be off by herself for a while. He said she'd been really strange and quiet lately, but I never noticed it. He said he was trying to get her to go see a doctor, but she wouldn't."

"Doesn't she have relatives or somebody you could call?" Don asked. "Parents or a sister? She might be hanging with her relatives."

"My grandparents are dead, but I called Aunt Eileen. That's my mom's only sister. She and my mom were really close," Neal said. "They went shopping together every Thursday. She said she hasn't seen my mom or heard from her either. I told my dad to call the police and report her as a missing person, but then he told me that he thinks she's at one of those women's shelters. He said she thinks he was verbally abusing her and that's what the whole thing is about. I guess they won't tell anybody where a woman is when they're at those places," Neal said.

"Was your dad verbally abusing your mom?" Carla asked.

"I don't know," Neal said. "I thought they were just arguing. I'm not sure."

There were many times when Don felt envious toward Neal with his brand-new car and his cushy job at the furniture store, but right now Don's heart went out to him. Don could not imagine how he would feel if his mother pulled a disappearing act like that. It would tear out his heart.

Neal looked at Don and Carla, a haunted look in his eyes. "Don't your parents ever fight?"

Carla laughed. "Big time. But my dad says the best part of it is making up again. My mom likes it too. He brings her all kinds of goodies," she said.

"My parents argue too," Don said. "They both get in their licks, but then they get together before nighttime. My mom has this rule. You never go to bed angry."

....

After school, Don took the items he had

found in Julio's desk to the police lieutenant who was investigating his brother's death. Grace Blake was a 35-year-old African-American officer with a no-nonsense style.

"I was going over my brother's things, and I found these in his desk," Don said, handing the items to the lieutenant.

Lieutenant Blake studied the items briefly, and then she looked up. "So, Julio had an appointment for that hour at the taco stand. Have you any idea who wrote either of these notes?" she asked.

"No. I'm not sure the letter from that woman was even addressed to Julio. Maybe it was meant for somebody else and he just picked it up," Don said. "I never heard of anybody called 'Space Girl.'"

"Well, this unsigned note really interests me," Lieutenant Blake said. "Apparently he had seen something that bothered him. He was thinking of going to the police, and this individual was pleading with him not to, asking for time. Thanks for bringing this in. We are going on the assumption that Julio was shot by mistake in a random killing, but if he had an appointment to be there at that precise time, well, then, it looks deliberate."

Lieutenant Blake had interviewed Don right after Julio died, and she kept asking him if he knew anybody who hated his brother enough to kill him. Don had to say that Julio was a guy without enemies because that was the truth. Don had not been able to come up with any reasonable motive why somebody would kill his brother. Nor could he now.

But now he thought that there was a motive. He and the police just didn't know what it was yet.

As Don drove home, he muttered to himself, "Julio, I wish you could tell me what happened. I wish you could send me a sign. What did you see that bothered you? What did you think you saw? Did anybody ever explain it to you?"

As Don turned onto his street, he glanced at a girl running brokenly down the street, holding a handkerchief to the side of her face.

It was Elena!

Don pulled to the curb and shouted, "Elena, what's the matter? Are you hurt?"

She stumbled over to the truck, her eyes red and wet. "Oh, Don," she wept.

Don opened the door, and she got in beside him.

"Elena, that *serpiente*, did he do this to you? Did Rattler hurt you again?" Don asked, staring at her bruised and bleeding cheek.

"Yes. I am through with him," Elena said bitterly.

"You've said that before," Don said.

"But this time I mean it," Elena said. "Julio was trying to help me get my GED so I could get a decent job and make something of myself, and now I'm going to do it. I'm going to take a class to prepare me for the GED. I can get somewhere like my sister. Julio told me I'm smart and I can make a good life if I want it. Now I believe everything he told me. Julio will help me from heaven where he is now."

"Elena, why did he beat you this time?" Don asked. "Was it because he saw me at your place?"

"No. He told me to come over to his place and make some steaks for his *loco* friends and him. I did, but the meat was very tough, so he got angry and started hitting me. He called me a fool and other things so terrible I can't repeat them. He has no respect for me. He started slapping me in the face. He slapped my face from side to side, and each time he slapped me he said, '*bobo*—stupid' and his friends laughed." Elena rolled up the sleeve of her blouse where a dark, angry bruise made her arm swell. "He told me he is going to take me over to 18th Street where the drug house is and give me to this big fat man they call Lizard Man, and he'll break my spirit for good. But it won't happen. I will never go near Ric again. Never."

"You have to call the police right now, Elena, and they'll arrest him for what he did to you. That's a crime," Don said.

"Oh, no. I couldn't do that," Elena said.

"Do you still care for him?" Don demanded.

"No. I hate him. We're finished. I told you. I never want to see him again," Elena said. "But I don't want to send him to jail. They wouldn't keep him there for very long, and he would get out and come after me. I shudder to think what he would do to me."

"Elena, do you think Ric killed Julio?" Don asked. "Do you think he knew Julio was trying to help you improve your life, and he saw that as taking you away from him?"

"No," Elena said. "I don't think Ric is mixed up in what happened to your brother. Ric is cruel, and I think he could kill somebody and sleep like a baby the night that he did it. But he had no reason to kill Julio. He did not know what Julio was trying to do for me. If he had known, he would have made fun of me and told me that I am so stupid that I would fail. But he never talked about it."

"Elena, I found out that Julio had seen something that looked very serious to him and he was thinking about going to the police about it. But then somebody wrote him a note offering to explain whatever it was," Don said.

"If Julio saw Ric doing something bad like that, he wouldn't have written a note offering to explain it. Ric can barely read and write," Elena said.

"Did you ever hear of a girl with the nickname 'Space Girl'?" Don asked. "Julio had a letter from her too."

Elena looked perplexed for a moment. Then a look of recognition came to her face. She nodded, "Yeah, I know who that is. When I ran into Julio at the mall one day, he told me he had to pick up some office supplies for Space Girl. I laughed and asked him who she was, and he said she was the bookkeeper at Harvey's Furniture Store. He said she had dropped out of high school years ago just like me, and then she got her GED. Now she has that great job making good money. He told me I should follow after her . . ."

Don knew the bookkeeper at Harvey's Furniture Store. Her name was Suzanna Wolf, and she was a stunning blond. "Suzanna Wolf?" Don asked. "Is that her?"

"Yes!" Elena said. "That was the name he mentioned."

Don wondered what there had been between Julio and Suzanna. Had she written that angry letter to Julio? Was he dating her and Tami? Julio surely did have an eye for pretty girls. He had more dates in his junior and senior years at Moreno High than anybody else. Underneath his senior class picture in the yearbook was the description "Heartbreaker of Moreno High."

5 DON HAD ONLY BEEN working at Harvey's Furniture Store for a month. Before that he had worked at a pizza place for about ten hours a week. The pay was poor, and they didn't give him enough hours. So he was grateful when Mr. Harvey agreed to give him his brother's job. Still, it grieved Don that he had this job because Julio no longer needed it.

In the time Don had worked at the store, he hadn't gotten to know Suzanna very well. She wasn't very friendly to the young movers. She was very pretty and sophisticated, maybe 27 or 28. It was hard to imagine Julio dating her. He was only 19, almost 20. But still, the letter she had signed "Space Girl" clearly indicated she was frustrated by a relationship the guy was neglecting, and Julio had the letter in his possession. If it wasn't directed to him, he must have found it somewhere and thought it was important enough to keep.

Don went to work as usual in the

afternoon, carrying furniture to the loading dock and placing it in trucks. Near quitting time he noticed that Suzanna was alone in the office, so he headed there. He dreaded talking to the woman, but he had to.

"Hi," Don said nervously, poking his head in the door of the office.

Suzanna was sitting in front of her computer, but Don could see that the computer was in sleep mode and Suzanna was doing her nails. "Hi," she responded with a quizzical look on her face.

"Do you have a minute to talk?" Don asked.

"Sure, why not?" she said in a breezy voice. Mr. Harvey had attended Julio's funeral, but Suzanna hadn't. Not that anyone expected her to. As far as Don knew then, she had little to do with Julio. He was just one of the kids working on the loading dock.

"Ms. Wolf, I'm Julio's brother, you know," he started out. "I've been, uh . . . sorting through his stuff, hoping to find something to help the police track his killer."

Suzanna looked more puzzled than ever. "And?" she said impatiently.

"I found this letter in his stuff," Don said, putting the copy of the letter from "Space Girl" before her. "I was wondering if you could help me figure this out."

Suzanna paled the moment she saw the letter. She dropped her nail file and almost spilled the little bottle of polish. Her eyes widened and her nostrils flared. "What has this got to do with me?" she demanded.

"Well, the letter is signed 'Space Girl' and, uh . . . somebody told me that's your nickname," Don said.

Suzanna crumpled up the letter in her hand. "This is just garbage!" she cried.

"Uh, that's just a copy of the original letter," Don said.

Her initial shock fading, Suzanna now glared at Don, "Just what are you trying to say to me? What's your angle?" she demanded.

"I told you. I'm trying to piece together my brother's last days so I can help the police find his murderer," Don said. "I found the letter in my brother's desk. I just thought maybe you guys were dating and you'd be able to tell me something helpful."

Suzanna laughed sharply. "You thought I

was dating your brother?" she said.

"Yeah, it sounded weird to me too. He was just a kid," Don said.

"The thought of me dating him is just so ridiculous I can't imagine it," Suzanna said. "Mr. Harvey hires all these stupid little punks. I can barely stand to get close enough to them to hand them their paychecks, much less date one of them!"

"So what is the letter all about?" Don asked.

Suzanna's eyes narrowed. "The letter? You know I don't have to sit here and be questioned by some 17-year-old mover! You know that, don't you?" she said.

"I'm sorry," Don said. "I just want to find out who killed my brother."

Suzanna sneered. "Oh, and you think I was madly in love with your brother and when he wouldn't commit to our relationship, I killed him. Is that what your demented little brain has come up with?"

"No, I never thought that," Don said.

"Well, for your information, your brother must have found that letter somewhere in this office and picked it up. It's part of an assignment I'm writing for a short story class I'm taking. It's fiction, stupid! It has nothing to do with anything, okay?" Suzanna said. "So all your little amateur sleuthing is for nothing."

"I'm sorry I bothered you," Don said, though he did not believe her.

"Well, you should be sorry. I am absolutely outraged that you would come in here and act as if I had something to do with your brother getting killed. Everybody knows what happened to your brother. You people have these gang wars all the time, and apparently he stepped on somebody else's turf, or whatever. Maybe he made a move on a rival gang member's girl. Your brother is just the latest casualty in these gang wars you people are so fond of." Suzanna's voice oozed with malice.

"My brother had nothing to do with gangs. He was an honor student. He was going to college to be a doctor," Don said.

"Oh, I'm sure," Suzanna said in a snide voice. "Guys like him don't get to be doctors. Drug dealers maybe, but not doctors."

"I resent that," Don snapped.

"Well, I resent you," she snapped back.

Don walked from the office trembling with anger. He could understand Suzanna being upset that he had asked her about the letter, but that didn't give her the right to trample on Julio's memory.

Don moved another truckload of furniture from the showroom before quitting time. Then as Don prepared to leave, Mr. Harvey called out to him, "Come into the office, Don."

When Don reached the office, he noticed Suzanna had gone home. Mr. Harvey was alone. "This is a week's payment. It will give you a chance to find something else," he said.

Don stared at the man. "You're firing me?" he asked.

"Well, we won't be needing you here anymore, Don. I, uh . . . made a mistake hiring you after your brother's . . . uh . . . passing. You are obviously too distraught over the matter to concentrate on your work. I am afraid I was acting out of misguided compassion. I think you need some time to . . . ah . . . grieve," Mr. Harvey said.

"But last week you told me I was the

best guy here," Don said. "That I did more work than anybody."

"Don, don't make it more difficult than it already is. I'm sure you'll find something else quickly. I'll give you a good recommendation," Mr. Harvey said.

"Suzanna is making you do this, isn't she?" Don asked.

"What? Ms. Wolf? This has nothing to do with my bookkeeper," Mr. Harvey said.

"I found a strange letter she had written in Julio's desk and I talked to her about it. I guess that made her mad enough to get me fired," Don said.

Mr. Harvey looked miserable. "Good luck, Don. Please let there be no hard feelings."

Don left the furniture store, his brain spinning. Why was Suzanna so freaked by that letter? Don didn't buy her story about it being a class assignment for a minute. Why did she get so upset that she had forced Mr. Harvey to fire Don over it?

The letter had to mean something important.

On his way home, Don drove over to Elena's house to check on her. He hoped she had meant it when she said she was breaking off with Rattler, but he wasn't so sure. Elena was pretty vulnerable.

When Don drove up to Elena's house, her little brother was skateboarding in the street. "Elena home?" Don shouted.

"Nope," the boy shouted back. "She went down to Moreno to see about some class or something."

It was almost 8:00 and dark. Don was glad that Elena was serious enough about getting her GED that she was enrolling already in the preparation class, but he was worried about her walking in the dark on these streets. "When did she leave?" he asked her brother.

"An hour ago. Something like that," the boy shouted.

Don drove toward Moreno High School. He planned to wait for Elena and give her a ride home when she came out of the class. Don watched for her as he drove.

When Don reached the high school, most of the students were already milling around outside. He searched for Elena in the crowd, but he didn't see her. He waited until everybody had cleared away. There was still no sign of her. Don was feeling nervous as he drove back to Elena's house.

Elena's older sister came to the door when Don knocked. "Oh, Don. Isn't Elena with you?" she asked.

"I went down to Moreno looking for her, but I didn't see her. I was going to give her a ride home. I don't like her walking around the streets at night," Don said.

Elena's older sister, Ana, frowned. "I'm scared now. Where is she? Ric Cortez has been calling the house all day. He has been threatening Mama and me. We told him to stop calling and that Elena doesn't want to see him anymore. He cursed us."

"You should have called the police," Don said.

"I know, but we were too afraid it would only make him madder. He has been terrorizing everybody for so long. He's such a bad man," Ana said.

"You should have gotten one of those restraining orders against him so he couldn't go near the house or Elena," Don said. But it was too late for that now. He had probably been parked down the street, watching the house. When Elena started walking toward the high school, he probably followed her. Maybe he sweet-talked her into getting into his car. Ric could be charming when he wanted to be. Or maybe he just dragged her into his car.

Whatever had happened, Don feared that Elena was with him now. "I'm going to look for Elena," Don told Ana. "If I don't find her quickly, you guys had better call the police."

Don could hear Elena's mother crying inside the house. Don shook his head sadly and returned to his truck. Elena was such a pretty girl. When she had attended Moreno High, she had earned good grades. She had a real flair for math. She had no problem with algebra when the rest of the class was sweating over the problems. She would've had a good future ahead of her if she hadn't met Rattler in her sophomore year. He bought her gifts and flattered her. Then he got her to drop out of school because he said he needed her all the time. And by the time she realized she had made a mistake, it was too late. It was like picking up a pretty red-and-yellow rope only to find out it was a deadly coral snake and its venom was already coursing through your body.

6 DON ROUNDED UP two friends, Matt Garcia and Luis Arguello, to drive to Rattler's apartment with him. Don didn't see Rattler's silver vintage Camaro parked anywhere nearby. When Don hit the doorbell, a muscular guy appeared. "Yeah?" he snapped.

"Is Ric around?" Don asked.

"Nah. Hey, you're Don Saenz. Your brother is the one who got offed, right?" the young man said.

Don ignored the question. "Is Elena Redondo here?" he asked.

"That crazy *muchacha*? Ric dumped her for keeps."

"When Ric gets back, you tell him that if Elena doesn't turn up okay, we're going to the police," Don said.

The guy's face hardened. "Hey, you talk tough for a boy!" he said. Other sinister-looking young men appeared behind him. Matt and Luis flanked Don, leaving no doubt that if trouble broke out, Don wouldn't be standing alone.

"Just give him the message," Don said, turning to go.

Back in Don's pickup, Matt grumbled, "What makes girls like Elena so stupid? I could have asked her out a hundred times, and the answer would have always been negative. How come they go for guys like Rattler?"

"Guys like him have lots of money," Luis said. "He can flash the jewelry and tickets to the hot concerts. That's what girls are looking for. They're materialistic, man."

"You're not kidding," Matt said bitterly. "They got dollar signs in their eyes."

"Carla isn't like that," Don said.

"Yeah, well most girls are," Luis said.

"Where does Rattler get his money anyway?" Matt asked. "He never works. I've never known him to have any kind of a job. He carries around a wallet bulging with money, and he's always driving a new car. Where's it coming from?"

"A lot of it comes from scaring people into paying protection money. The guy I used to work for, Mr. Harvey, he's been paying Rattler for years. It's like a regular thing. If he doesn't, Rattler makes sure his windows are busted. Garbage is dumped in his parking lot in the middle of the night," Don said.

"And he does hits too," Luis said.

Don had never heard that before. "What do you mean, 'hits,' Luis?" Don asked.

"He'll beat a guy up for somebody. You know, if the guy owes money and isn't paying up. He'll maybe do even worse than that. I'm not sure, but I heard rumors that he'll do anything if the price is right," Luis said.

"Where did you hear that?" Don asked.

"My older brother. He went through a time when he was a wannabe gang member, and one time Rattler told him there was real good money in the deal, especially if you got lucky and somebody wanted a guy put under the grass. He said you could get really rich that way," Luis said.

"Maybe Rattler was just shooting off his mouth," Don said.

"Maybe," Luis allowed, "but maybe not. I wouldn't put anything past the guy."

They drove up one street and down another looking for Elena. Then, around 9:00, they spotted Ric's Camaro cruising down the street. Don gained on it in his rusty old pickup and then pulled up alongside at a light.

"Hey, Ric, you see Elena?" Don shouted.

Ric turned and grinned. "Who? I don't know anybody by that name."

"Come on, man," Don yelled, "you want me to graze that nice silver Camaro with my truck here?" If there was anything to strike terror in Rattler's heart, it was damage to his fancy cars.

"I heard she's partying with her friends," Rattler yelled back, speeding up and threading his way through traffic and away from Don's truck. Something about Rattler's evil smirk sparked a memory. Elena's frightened voice echoed in his brain.

He told me he is going to take me over to 18th Street where the drug house is and give me to this big fat man they call Lizard Man and he'll break my spirit for good . . .

Suddenly Don hit the accelerator, and the truck took off.

"What's happening, man?" Matt asked.

"I just remembered something," Don said. "I think I know where Elena is."

When they pulled up in front of the house on 18th Street, they heard music blasting from the open doors and windows. There was definitely a party going on. People were dancing on the dirt front yard and yelling. Don could tell that some of them were already pretty high.

"Elena might be here," Don said.

They parked and got out. Then they stood on the fringe of the party, looking for Elena. Don spotted her first. Her hair was in disarray, and she was clearly under the influence of something. Maybe she was drunk, or maybe it was something else.

"Hey, Elena," Don shouted. "What's the matter with you? What are you doing here?"

"Hi, Don," Elena said in a slurred voice. She tried to walk toward him, but she was unsteady on her feet. She stumbled and fell.

Don walked over, taking her hand and pulling her to her feet. "Your mom is worried about you, Elena. You've got to get out of here."

A mean-looking heavy man whose body was crisscrossed with tattoos of lizards intercepted them. *Lizard Man*. The guy Rattler had threatened Elena with. "Hey, dude, don't mess with my girl, if you know what's good for you," he growled.

"Man, she's 15 years old," Don lied. "You don't want that kind of trouble."

Elena was 18, but she would have easily passed for 15 with her slight frame and baby face.

"Fifteen!" Lizard Man gasped. He cursed then and walked away.

Don led Elena back toward the pickup. "What happened, Elena?" he asked her.

"I don't know," she cried. The cool night air was slapping her face, sobering her a little.

"You were supposed to be registering for a GED prep class at Moreno. How did you get over here?" Don asked.

Luis and Matt jumped in the bed of the pickup while Don put the girl in the seat beside him. She was crying hard now, her shoulders shaking. Slowly, brokenly, the story came out. "Ric stopped. I was walking to school. He said he'd give me a lift. He said it was okay that I didn't want to be his girlfriend anymore. He was really nice. He said I should go get my GED. He said it was okay, so I got in the car with him, but he didn't go to Moreno."

"Where did you go?" Don asked, starting the pickup.

"We stopped and bought some sodas in a little store. He must have put something in mine. I was laughing so hard I couldn't stop. I felt so weird . . . I got hysterical, and then Ric got really mean. He slapped me and said he'd show me what happened to girls who played games with him. I asked him to take me home, but he just slapped me again. Then he took me to the drug house on 18th Street. He dragged me inside and told Lizard Man that I needed some lessons in how to be nice. Ric told me I belonged on 18th Street, that I was nothing but garbage and I'd never get my GED," Elena said.

"*Serpiente*," Don said bitterly.

"Somebody has got to get that guy," Luis said through the open window that connected the cab to the bed of the pickup. "Somebody has got to stop him."

"Yeah, lots of luck," Matt said.

Don dropped Matt and Luis off at their houses. Then he took Elena home.

Elena's mother and sister rushed outside when they saw Elena in the truck. Don told them what had happened. "There's a 24-hour emergency room down at the clinic," Don said. "You should take her there. It's not that far. She needs a doctor to look her over. She's been punched and slapped around, and she's got some drugs in her system."

Don left Elena with her family and then headed home.

"Don!" his dad cried when he saw his son. "It's after midnight!"

His mom was in the living room saying her rosary. "*Hijo*," she cried. "I have said four rosaries!"

"Good," Don said. "They worked. I got Elena home safe. Everything is okay."

"Don," Dad said gravely, "this family has already suffered a great tragedy losing Julio. Our hearts will never heal from that wound. You must not endanger your life too. Look at what it has done to your mother!"

"I'm sorry," Don said, sitting down on the living room sofa and putting his arm around his mother's shoulders. "Mr. Harvey fired me from the furniture store today."

"Fired you?" his dad cried. "What for?"

"I guess his bookkeeper was angry that I was asking her questions about Julio. I am trying to find out all I can so I can help the police with their investigation," Don said. "But I can get another job easy. Matt works over at the electronics store, and he can get me in there. I can make better money, commissions even."

"*Hijo*," his dad said, "what is this about helping the police with their investigation? This is not your business. Julio is with God, and nobody can bring him back to us on this earth. You are risking your own life going around like a chicken with its head cut off asking dangerous questions and stirring up trouble."

"Yeah, well, I'm being very careful," Don said. "I'm going to bed now."

Don walked down the hall and quickly showered. When he was in his robe, heading for bed, Josefina appeared in her pajamas.

"You okay, Don?" she asked in a small voice.

"Sure, *cosa dulce*," Don said, opening his arms as the little girl leaped into them. He gave her a big hug, like Julio used to do. Josefina was born when Julio was 9 and Don was 7. She was a very big thing in their lives. They were so excited about this baby girl joining the family, and they treated her like a princess. Don knew that Josefina missed Julio as much as he did.

"I heard Mama crying, and I was so scared," Josefina said. "She was worried when you didn't come home. She was scared something bad would happen to you like it happened to Julio."

Don hugged the little girl tighter. He could understand her terror. Julio had left that evening with everything appearing to be normal. Then the police came to the door and their lives changed forever. They were told that Julio was in the ER at General Hospital, and they knew from the somber attitude of the officer that the situation was desperate. Julio was dead on arrival at the hospital.

"I'm being real careful, Josie," Don promised. "I'm not going anywhere. I'll always be here for you. When you grow up and get married, I'll be there wishing you happiness."

"I don't ever want to get married," Josefina said.

"It's too early to decide that," Don said. "You're only 10."

"I don't care," Josefina said. "I want to always live with you and Mom and Dad, and I don't want anything to change ever."

Josefina went back to bed after two more hugs from Don.

In his own bed, Don glanced across the room to the small table on which was mounted the color photograph of Julio. It was his senior picture from Moreno High School. The little light flickered in the darkness.

"Who killed you, Julio?" Don asked sorrowfully. "Who took you away from us too soon? I wish you could give me a clue, brother."

The questions swirled in Don's mind, keeping him from sleep. He felt like he had a big jigsaw puzzle mostly done, but important pieces were missing. He had to find those pieces. When he put them in place, he would know who killed Julio.

7 AT SCHOOL THE NEXT DAY, Neal seemed really uncomfortable when his gaze met Don's. Don felt sorry for the guy having to deal with his mother disappearing. Lately he was getting a lot of consolation from hanging with Don and his friends, but since his father had fired Don, Don figured he didn't feel comfortable joining the group as usual. So when Don, Carla, and Matt sat down in the cafeteria, Neal seemed reluctant to come over.

"Hey, Neal," Don called out. "There's room over here."

Neal hurried over with his tray. "Hey, man," he said to Don, "I'm really sorry about what happened at the store."

"Yeah," Carla said, "your father fired Don, huh?" She drove her fork into an asparagus spear. Lately, the school cafeteria was on a vegetable kick, including broccoli and asparagus in the daily fare.

"It's not your fault, Neal," Don said. "Don't sweat it."

"That Suzanna Wolf," Neal said bitterly,

"she's a wolf all right. I can't stand her. She stabbed you in the back, Don."

Don was surprised at the venom in Neal's voice. Why was he so upset about Don getting fired?

"She's a real gold digger," Neal continued. "She'd like to get on my dad's good side now, you know, marry him and stuff, and get all the money he and my mom made. She's been married twice already. She's like 30, and my dad's 57, so he's really excited that a pretty, younger woman is interested in him. You don't know how awful it is around my house now. It's bad enough my mom being gone and everything, but my dad has got that woman hanging around like they're already married or something."

"That really stinks," Carla said, stabbing another asparagus spear. "Tell him you're going to flunk school and become a delinquent if he doesn't act his age. Maybe that'll scare him."

"Yeah," Matt laughed. "Get to be a real problem kid. That'll shake him up."

"You know what," Don said. "I found this letter in Julio's desk. It is signed 'Space Girl,' and that's Suzanna's nickname.

Well, it was a really nasty letter, and she was accusing some guy of playing games, jerking her around. The letter wasn't addressed to Julio, but he had it . . . I wonder, could Julio have been hanging out with Suzanna?"

Neal made a face. "That's what she calls herself all right, 'Space Girl.' That's because she's so good at the new technology. Like a new computer program needs to be installed, and she's on top of it right away. But Julio never seemed to even notice her."

"Oh, I bet he noticed her," Matt cut in. "What guy wouldn't? I went in the furniture store with my dad, and his eyes were popping out of his head when he spotted her. Mine were too."

"Yeah, but Julio was dating Tami Ferraro," Don said. "He was even bringing Tami to family things. Julio wasn't the kind of a guy who'd be dating two girls at once. He had too much honor for that, you know."

Neal shrugged. "Suzanna acts much younger than she is. She's always bragging about having to be carded when she goes to buy liquor. But I never saw Julio talking really friendly to her or anything. Unless they kept it out of the store. Sometimes she'd flirt with him, like she does with a lot of guys, but he'd seem to just brush it off," he said.

"You guys are such pushovers for pretty girls," Carla said. "It's like your heads are on swivels or something. Let some cute little thing go by and you almost fall over your own feet. Even you, Don. You can be walking at the mall and this little short dress with the stiletto heels comes along and whoa, your eyeballs jump right out of your face."

"That's not true," Don said.

"Sure it is," Carla laughed. "You know what I think? I'd make a law that guys have to wear blinders like horses used to. You know, these leather flaps on either side of their head so they can just look straight ahead. That way you wouldn't throw your necks out of joint looking at every girl."

Don was annoyed. They were acting as if Julio was some creep who had two girls on the string. Don knew better. "Hey, I know my brother," he said. "He had a huge amount of honor. He wouldn't have been fooling around with somebody else when he was going with Tami."

"Well, you're the one who asked about it," Carla pointed out. "Anyway, don't make a saint out of him, Don. He was a wonderful guy, but he was human just like the rest of us. We all have our flaws and weaknesses."

"Yeah," Neal chimed in. "I'm doing that with my mom. She nagged a lot and she was such a perfectionist that it drove me crazy sometimes. But I don't think of any of that anymore. Now that she's gone, I'm just remembering the great things about her. I'm just missing her so much, and all I can think of are the really cool things she did to make my life better. I know it sounds stupid, but nobody loves me as much as my mom . . . nobody, and I miss that!"

"But it's not like she's dead, Neal," Carla said. "She'll be back. She's probably at one of those women's shelters where they have group sessions and dis their husbands and stuff. You know, where women go when they're just so fed up with everything that they can't take it anymore. My mom is always threatening to go to one of those places, but then she has six kids so I guess she's entitled to be a little crazy sometimes."

....

Later on that day Don had a test in Mr. Foxworth's class. Don had forced himself to study for it. He had drilled himself over and over on all the factors that had led to World War II, the way mistakes were made after World War I, making the next war inevitable. How the world stupidly ignored Hitler's evil until it was too late.

But now, as he looked at the essay question, Don was drawing a blank.

"How did appeasement play a role in the rise of Hitler's Germany until a world conflict was inevitable?" the question asked. Suddenly Don started writing, remembering what he had studied. But while he was writing about how a frightened, naive world was ignoring Hitler and allowing him to become more dangerous in their midst, he was actually thinking of Rattler in his own neighborhood. The same thing, on a smaller scale, was happening where Don lived.

Nobody had ever been willing to stand up to Rattler and stop him. The first time he threatened the widow who ran the little vegetable stand, everybody should have banded together against him. But the lady was alone, so she paid the blackmail money. She couldn't have Rattler and his friends come by, smash her fresh tomatoes, and take away her small margin of profit. And then others paid. Mr. Harvey not only paid, but he made sure to be very cordial to Rattler and his friends when they came around to collect. Julio used to tell Don how sick it made him to see Mr. Harvey treating the criminals as if they were legitimate business people.

The first time Rattler slapped a girlfriend around, her father and brothers, and all the other fathers and brothers, should have gotten together and run him out of the neighborhood. Even now, after what Elena had suffered at Rattler's hands, her mother and sister would not go to the police. They would not file a restraining order against Rattler. They preferred to cower in their house and hope Rattler was done trampling on Elena. They hoped he would now, finally, leave her alone.

Don wrote furiously, passionately. He wrote about the British diplomat, who went, hat in hand, to make a deal with Hitler, certain that if he threw the tyrant one more small country then Hitler would at last be satisfied. About how the diplomat, clutching his umbrella and smiling hopefully, announced to the gullible world that because he had appeased Hitler, there would be peace in our time.

But Don was writing about Rattler too. Deep in his heart, Don was sure that Rattler had killed Julio. He did not yet know why, but he was sure he had done it.

Don turned in his test. Then he walked outside into the cloudy afternoon. Why wouldn't Tami talk to him? he wondered. She was so grief-stricken at the funeral. Why wouldn't she spare him a few minutes thinking it might help find Julio's killer?

Don tried calling Tami again, but he always got her voice mail. He figured caller ID prevented him from ever getting through to Tami. So in desperation, Don got her address from Julio's book, and in the early evening he drove to her place.

She lived in a cluster of nice apartments on a tree-lined street. Except for the distant barking of a dog, it was peaceful and quiet in this neighborhood.

Don went to her door and rang the bell. Tami opened the peephole in the door and said, "Yes?"

"Hi. I'm really sorry to bother you again, but I need to talk to you for just a few minutes," Don said.

"I told you I didn't want to go over it all again," Tami groaned.

"Please," Don said.

The girl sighed. Then she unlocked the deadbolt. The door opened. She was a thin, pale girl with long straight hair and eyes that looked too big for her face. He remembered her from the barbecue as more vivacious, prettier. "Come in if you must," she said.

"Thank you," Don said, sitting on the sofa opposite her. Her apartment was nice, but far from luxurious.

"My roommate isn't home yet," Tami said. "Please be gone before she gets home."

"This won't take long. I just wondered if

you knew about Suzanna Wolf," Don said.

Tami rolled her eyes. "Yes, of course."

Don swallowed hard. He hoped it wasn't true after all that Julio was dating both girls. That would have been really awful. "Did she mean anything to Julio? Could you tell me that?" he asked, dreading the answer.

"He disliked her. She worked in the furniture store with him. There was bad blood between them, really bad blood," Tami said. "But please, don't get any crazy idea that she had anything to do with . . . harming Julio. It was nothing like that. It was just that Julio could not stand to see people getting hurt, and Suzanna was trying to break up his boss's marriage. Julio felt sorry for the wife. A poor, wimpy woman without a clue as to what was happening, I guess."

"Suzanna was after Mr. Harvey?" Don asked.

"Yes. It's nothing original. He has lots of money, investments. She smelled money, and she wanted it. Julio was so big-hearted that he thought he could fix things. He thought he could talk to the man and tell him to do the honorable thing! Can you imagine such a thing? A 19-year-old lecturing some fat, balding man about morals?" Tami said, shaking her head.

"Did he talk to Mr. Harvey?" Don asked.

"I begged him not to. I told Julio to mind his own business," Tami said. "But he talked to Mr. Harvey, and I guess the man's affair with Suzanna cooled a little. Then she wrote this bitter letter to Mr. Harvey, kind of threatening him to leave unless he made some decision in her favor."

The letter! So it was to Mr. Harvey! Julio must have found it.

"I saw that letter," Don said. "It was in Julio's desk."

"Yes, Julio got it before Mr. Harvey saw it. Julio was so determined to save poor Mrs. Harvey's failing marriage." Tami shook her head again. "He was such a sweet, good guy. So incredible. He was too good for this world, I guess." Tears started in the girl's eyes and trickled down her face. "I'll never find another guy like him. Never. I lost so much. We were starting to make plans. We were talking about getting married when we finished college."

She dabbed at her eyes with a tissue, then pulled herself together and stared at Don impassively. As if she had decided she had to get over it. She had to.

8 DON WAS REALLY SORRY he had had to upset Tami again, but at least now he knew the letter had not been addressed to Julio. When Neal had mentioned that his father was now with Suzanna so much, it had crossed Don's mind that maybe the relationship had started even before Mrs. Harvey disappeared. Maybe, in fact, that is why she left. When she finally realized her husband did not love her anymore, she probably lost it. She just had to get away, even from her beloved son. Women whose longtime marriages break up sometimes do crazy things.

On Saturday morning, Don returned to the Colorado Taco Shop as he had done many times since Julio's death. The police had questioned everybody in the vicinity, but Julio kept hoping that there was someone who had been missed, someone with a clue. Now, once again, he crossed the street to the three-story senior citizens apartments. He saw two ladies walking on Madison. He had talked to the taller of the pair before, but he hadn't met her companion before.

"You're the young man who lost the brother," the tall woman said sympathetically. "Bea, this is the boy I told you about. His brother was shot over in front of the taco shop that night."

"Yes, ma'am," Don said, "I'm still talking to people, hoping somebody saw something they haven't reported yet."

Bea frowned and shuddered. "I was visiting Aline that night when the shooting happened. I haven't been back since, until today. I was so frightened. I heard the shots, and oh, I just panicked," she said.

"Bea insisted on going home right away. We called a cab to take her home," Aline said. "I tried to tell her that terrible things happen all over, but she swore she would never come back to this street."

"Did you see anything that night that you might not have told the police?" Don asked Bea.

"Oh, I didn't talk to the police at all. I was gone by the time they started talking to people. But I didn't see anything that would have helped, anyway. I'm sure a young man did the shooting. Young men always do these kinds of shootings. The only unusual thing I saw was this middle-aged man down the street sitting in his BMW and sweating profusely. Our cab went right by him. I thought he was having a heart attack."

Don stared at Bea. "A BMW in this neighborhood?" he asked. The only people he knew around here who drove BMWs were the Harveys. "What did he look like?"

"Just an ordinary-looking white man. Except he had some sort of red birthmark on his face. I looked right at him," Bea said.

Shock went through Don's mind.

"Thank you so much, ma'am," he said. He had begun to shake.

Don knew where he had to go. He headed to Harvey's Furniture Store. He walked inside and strode to the office where Mr. Harvey was sitting at his computer. He wasn't very good at the computer, but he was learning. Suzanna had been teaching him, but she wasn't there now.

"Oh, Don," Mr. Harvey said a little sheepishly. "How are you doing? Do you have a job yet?"

"No, not yet. That's what I came about. You said you'd write a letter of recommendation for me. I thought maybe you could do that now. It wouldn't have to be long. Just a short letter would be fine. I could wait right here for it," Don said.

"Of course. I could do that," Mr. Harvey said, apparently relieved that this was not going to be some unpleasant meeting between him and an irate ex-employee. He turned to his typewriter and slid in stationery with the name of the furniture store. He still wasn't adept enough on the computer to do the job there. So he relied on a small electric typewriter for correspondence.

Mr. Harvey typed the two-paragraph letter of recommendation and handed it to Don. "I hope this helps."

"Thank you very much," Don said.

Don couldn't wait to get back to his pickup. He took out the copy of the note addressed to Julio asking him not to call the police, to wait for an explanation instead.

After carefully comparing the typing on both items, he found a similarity. The o was dirty and clogged.

It looked like the same typewriter had been used.

Don's heart raced. Mr. Harvey had written that note to Julio asking him to wait for an explanation before he called the police about something.

Maybe Mr. Harvey was cooking the books and Julio had stumbled onto it. Maybe he was cheating on his income taxes. But, no, Julio would have had no way of finding that out. Besides, Julio wouldn't have gotten involved in something like that. Julio only cared about people. That's why he was trying to save Mrs. Harvey's marriage. He didn't want to see the lady hurt.

Of course, Julio must have seen that something was going on between Mr. Harvey and his bookkeeper. Tami said he knew about it and was trying to smooth things over. Maybe Julio had come to the store after a late-night delivery and had surprised Mr. Harvey and Suzanna. Maybe something had happened . . . or maybe Julio had surprised Mr. Harvey and his wife. Maybe there had been an argument, and Mr. Harvey even got so angry that he slapped his wife. Mr. Harvey was a mild-mannered man most of the time, but when he lost his temper, he could be dangerous. He once punched a teenaged mover and almost got hit with a lawsuit. He had to pay the family off. If Julio had seen Mr. Harvey hitting his wife, he might have threatened to call the police. He might have stormed out. Maybe Mr. Harvey quickly typed the note and ran after him, handing it to him as a sort of promise that he would explain the situation and clear things up.

Don decided that he had to talk to Mrs. Harvey. She was hiding out somewhere, but surely someone knew where she was. She had to have friends who had an idea how to get in touch with her. She probably told one of them where she was going. Women usually had at least one confidante. Don knew his mother had several friends, and sometimes she told them things she did not even share with her family.

Don called Neal and asked him to meet him at a hamburger house near Moreno High.

"What's up?" Neal wanted to know.

"It's real important. I'll tell you when you get here," Don said.

In 20 minutes, Neal was walking into the small restaurant. He spotted Don in a booth and came over. "What's going on, man?" he asked.

"I need to talk to your mom, Neal. I found out some things today, and it's really important that I talk to her. I think she can fill in some pieces of the puzzle and help me find out who killed Julio," Don said.

"What?" Neal cried, almost knocking over the soda he ordered. "What's my mom got to do with Julio's murder?"

"Neal, I found a note your father wrote to my brother telling Julio that he could explain everything. It said that Julio shouldn't call the police without waiting for an explanation. The note was weird. It said stuff. I think Julio stumbled onto something your parents were mixed up in and he wanted to report it, but your father talked him out of it. Maybe your mom was involved in the stuff too, and that's why she ran away. Maybe she was scared of the police getting involved," Don said. "I need to talk to her now."

"But I don't know where she is, Don. Even my dad doesn't know. I keep asking him if he's heard anything, and he says no," Neal said.

"Did your mom have any close friends?" Don asked.

"Yeah, Madge Amsterdam was one. She and my mom played cards. And my mom always went shopping on Friday with Lucy Briggs. That's when the stores have the big sales, and they never missed going. My mom has plenty of money, but she loves bargains," Neal said. "But we've called those women, and neither of them have heard a word from my mom."

"That sounds impossible," Don said. "Maybe they're just protecting her. Maybe they don't want her family bothering her for a while."

"I don't know. Lucy Briggs is real upset. She's always crying when we call her. She says my mom is like a sister to her," Neal said.

"Neal, tell me exactly what happened when your mom disappeared," Don asked. "Try to remember the details."

"Nothing much to tell," Neal said. "I was at school. It was Thursday. I came home after football practice at 5:00, and my dad was sitting in the living room looking really stunned. He had an awful look on his face. He said, 'Your mother left us. She packed all her clothes and left us.' I was totally shocked," Neal recalled.

"Was she normal in the morning before you went to school?" Don asked.

"Well, you know, she often slept late. I'd get my own breakfast. Put a bagel in the microwave, some cream cheese. I didn't see her Thursday morning at all, but my dad was there drinking his coffee. He would've said something if she'd been acting strange. So I guess in the morning, she didn't let on what she was going to do," Neal said.

"So when was the last time you saw her?" Don asked.

"Uh . . . Wednesday. She was going to get her hair done, and then she was going down to the furniture store because she said she wanted to talk to my dad about something. She took the trolley because then she wouldn't have to worry about her car. I was sleeping when they got home

Wednesday night because I didn't hear them get in. But my dad said they got home around 11:00. I guess the last time I saw her would be Wednesday morning. She seemed okay then," Neal said.

Don nodded. He tried to imagine the scenario. Mrs. Harvey disappeared between Wednesday morning and Thursday night. Julio was murdered on Friday night.

"And you say your father said she took all her clothes?" Don asked.

"Well, yeah, the stuff she liked and used all the time. Her makeup and stuff like that too. He said it must have taken her a while to pack," Neal said.

"Neal, where's your father now?" Don asked.

"At the store, I guess. Why? What are you driving at, Don?" Neal asked nervously.

"Would you take me to your house so we can look in your mom's bedroom, Neal?" Don asked.

"Uh, my dad wouldn't like that," Neal said. "He doesn't even go in their bedroom anymore since she's gone. He, uh . . . sleeps in the guest bedroom downstairs. He's kept the door closed since she left. I don't think he'd want us going in there."

"We have to, Neal. I think it will help you find where your mother is, and it might help me find out who killed Julio. I think we need to do it. Trust me, man. We'll go out there and take a quick look, and then we'll take off. Nobody needs to know, okay?" Don said.

Finally, Neal nodded, though he still looked nervous about it. "Okay, Don. Just in and out though. I don't want to be messing around that room and have my dad come home. He's got a bad temper. I don't want him taking it out on me."

Don followed Neal's new Accord to the beautiful upscale neighborhood where the Harveys lived. They had to drive up several winding roads with lyrical names before ending up on Whispering Palm Circle.

The home was a two-story sun-splashed Mediterranean that sprawled over an acre of beautifully kept lawn and gardens. Don was shocked. He knew that Mr. Harvey was prosperous, but he had no idea he was doing this well.

Neal led Don to the big master bedroom,

and, with trembling hands, he unlatched the door.

Everything looked pristine, like they were waiting for photographers from some gracious-living magazine to come and photograph the elegant room.

Don walked to the large closet and slid the door open. The closet was jammed with clothing, more clothing than Don had ever seen in his life, outside department stores.

"Are these your mom's?" he asked.

"Yeah, she liked clothes. She's always buying new ones," Neal said.

"So what's missing?" Don asked.

"Uh, she kept the clothes she really liked and wore all the time in this corner . . . like these black slacks . . . and the pullovers. She always wore these pullovers. Here's her jeans, the kind she liked . . ." Neal's voice started to crack. He began grabbing at the outfits with an almost frantic energy. "She left her jeans and tees . . . she left the pullovers."

"Is *anything* gone that you can see?" Don asked softly.

Neal didn't answer. He kept grabbing at his mother's favorite pieces of clothing, growing distraught. "Don . . . she . . . *didn't take anything*," he finally gasped.

9 DON DROVE ALONE to Harvey's Furniture Store early Sunday morning. The store opened at 8:00, and Don arrived ten minutes earlier. There were no customers in the store, and Mr. Harvey was back in the office.

"Hello," Don called to him.

"Oh, hello, Don. Did the letter of recommendation help you out?" Harvey asked cheerfully.

"Everything is fine. May I talk to you?" Don asked.

Mr. Harvey looked perplexed. "What about?" he asked.

"I think I told you how I'm trying to help the police solve my brother's murder," Don said.

"Uh . . . yes," Mr. Harvey said. Perhaps it was just Don's imagination, but it seemed that a sheen of perspiration suddenly appeared on the man's face.

"I think somebody hired a hit on Julio because he knew too much about something. I think Rattler Cortez may have been the hit man," Don said.

Mr. Harvey grabbed the arms of his swivel chair so tightly that his hands were soon bloodless. His face paled so that the birthmark stood out more sharply than usual. He held his breath for a moment. Then he slowly exhaled. "What has this got to do with me, Don? I don't understand."

"I talked to some people at the senior citizens apartments across from the Colorado Taco Shop where Julio got hit. One lady said she saw a man in a BMW sitting down the street from the place. He was looking directly at the spot where Julio got hit," Don said.

Tiny rivulets of perspiration now streamed down the fat man's cheeks and glistened on the bald spot on his head. "Surely you don't think for a minute that it was me. I'm not the only person in town with a BMW," he said.

"Yeah, but the lady said the man had a birthmark, and you don't see many people with that kind of a birthmark," Don said. "You see, Mr. Harvey, I was just wondering if you were actually there, maybe you saw who it was that shot Julio. According to what the lady said, you had a clear view of the place."

"It was not me. I was home in bed at the time your brother was shot," Mr. Harvey stammered.

"At 9:00 on a Friday night you're home in bed?" Don asked.

"I had a migraine," Mr. Harvey said, now sweating profusely.

"Well," Don said, "I've got a pretty good idea that Rattler was the one who shot my brother. I'm going to see the police now, and they'll bring him in for questioning. If I know anything about that cowardly little weasel, when the heat gets turned on, he'll sing like a canary. Rattler Cortez isn't going to take the rap by himself. No way. Whoever hired him is going to be right there beside him, facing first-degree murder charges."

Mr. Harvey looked like he was swimming in his own perspiration now. He kept tugging at the collar of his shirt. He got up from his chair and staggered visibly. It was clear that he was terrified.

"You okay, Mr. Harvey?" Don asked. "You don't look so good. Should I call somebody?"

"No," the man croaked. "I need to clear some things up here. I'm really busy."

"All right," Don said. "I just wanted to see if you had anything to add to the story before I go to the police."

Don left the furniture store and drove off. He parked down the road, in an alley. It gave him a good view of the parking lot behind the furniture store. Don watched for about ten minutes. Then he saw Mr. Harvey come rushing from the store, climb into his BMW, and take off.

Don followed the BMW for a short distance, just long enough to establish in his own mind that the man was not heading home. Don's words had frightened him so much that he no doubt had emptied the safe in the store and was now bound for the International Airport.

Don did not yet know what terrible secret Julio had stumbled on, what awful truth needed so badly to be concealed that a young man had to be executed to silence him.

But Don had begun to guess, and he had to stop Mr. Harvey from getting out of the country.

10 DON CALLED Lieutenant Blake on his cell phone and told her his theory. He gave her the make and license number of Mr. Harvey's car, and he told her the route he was taking that would end up at the airport. "I think he's going to flee the country because he did something bad. Julio suspected he had done it, but he hired a hit on Julio before he could talk. I think Ric Cortez did the shooting," Don said.

Don turned his pickup truck home then. He thought of his family. He knew he shouldn't try to take the law into his own hands. His family couldn't stand it if something happened to him. He was exhausted and tense. Maybe he had it figured all wrong, but he didn't think so. He still didn't have all the pieces of the jigsaw puzzle yet, but he was pretty certain what they looked like.

The police took Ric Cortez into custody at about the same time that Mr. Harvey was picked up at Los Angeles International

Airport. Ric stayed cool as ice, but Mr. Harvey immediately broke like an egg dropped from a tall building. He went totally to pieces, thinking Cortez was telling the whole story in another room.

Don's instincts had been correct. Wednesday night, the Harveys had had a terrible argument in the office of the furniture store. Mrs. Harvey had received a phone call from Suzanna asking her to grant her husband a divorce so he could find happiness with Suzanna. Mr. Harvey insisted that his wife had struck him first and he was only defending himself when he struck her over the head with his iron-tipped walking stick. Unfortunately, the blow was fatal.

Julio returned to the store late Wednesday night to find blood in the office. Mr. Harvey was rushing between the office and his BMW parked outside. He had pinned a note on the office door, knowing Julio was due back and would let himself in with a key even if the doors were locked.

Julio—I can explain everything. It's

not what you think. Leave the police out of it for now. Please. I'll explain everything.

Julio took the note and waited for Mr. Harvey. The man said he had cut his hand badly during an argument with his wife. He told Julio his wife had driven off in her car in a mad rage.

But Julio had expected the worst. The office was full of blood, and Mrs. Harvey was nowhere around. He should have called the police immediately. But he waited. Mr. Harvey had promised that he and his wife would meet Julio Friday evening at the Colorado Taco Shop and tell him what had happened. Harvey told Julio his wife was very embarrassed by the whole episode, and she wanted to buy Julio supper for causing him such distress.

"But," Carla said as Don told her the story, "why did Mr. Harvey put a hit on Julio?"

"Because Mr. Harvey knew when Friday night came he couldn't produce his wife. She was lying dead in the trunk of the BMW, wrapped in a garbage bag. Julio wouldn't have bought the story that she had disappeared. He saw the blood. He would have gone to the police. So Mr. Harvey got the worst guy he knew to shoot Julio," Don said sadly. "That gave Mr. Harvey time to bury Mrs. Harvey in the San Bernardino Mountains while everybody thought she had run away."

....

Mrs. Harvey's sister came down from Arcadia to live with Neal in the big house on Whispering Palm Circle. For a long time, Neal was in a state of shock, and it looked as if he wouldn't make it. But his friends helped him a lot. Don, Carla, Matt, and Luis stuck pretty close to him. And so when they planted the memorial jacaranda tree for Julio Anthony Saenz on the campus of Moreno High School, Neal was there in the circle with the rest, hands joined. Everybody cried a little and exchanged stories of Julio. They even laughed at some of the funny things he had done. And they began to heal. It wouldn't come overnight. But at least they had begun.